TIMELESS VOYAGE

CORNELIA AMIRI

TIMELESS VOYAGE Copyright © 2014 CORNELIA AMIRI

Cover art by Julie Darcy

Originally Published as TIMELESS VOYAGE 28 Days of Heart Series Copyright © 2010 CORNELIA AMIRI – by All Romance eBooks publication February 2010

ABOUT TIMELESS VOYAGE

Neither centuries that have come and gone nor the seas between us can keep us apart.

As the Celtic pirate, Anwen, presses her hard iron dagger against the Roman's throat, memories of fated lovers, druids, and sacrifice, stay her hand.

Kaeso is captivated by dreams of the woman he loved in a previous life, the mirror image of Anwen. In this lifetime they are foes, Roman and Celt. Can Anwen and Kaeso steer their timeless voyage to a happy destiny, or will they be robbed of love once more?

ONE

Off the coast of Ireland, 67 AD

BITING down on the dagger in her mouth, ignoring the bitter, metallic taste, Anwen glared at the swan prow of the Roman ship her crew rowed toward.

Delbaeth clutched a rowan firebrand at her side, veiling them in a cloud of dark, misty smoke, clogging her throat and stinging her eyes.

Blinking, Anwen dug her fingers into a soft leather pouch hanging from her belt, pinched a smooth lead pellet, and loaded the leather sling. Her men stroked their paddles through the briny water until the *curragh* bumped the side of the merchant ship. A shudder shot through her as icy water splashed her feet.

Delbaeth thrust the rowan torch into the Erinn Sea.

Anwen drew in a deep breath, sighted a Roman, and took aim, twirling the leather sling over her head in a lingering cloud of misty smoke. The iron pellet embedded in the sailor's forehead, sending him backwards as he fell to his death.

"Good shot, Captain." Delbaeth threw his dagger at another Roman. It struck the screaming man just below his neck.

Anwen's heart lurched in her chest as she clambered onto the deck. A burly, bearded man rushed toward her. Grabbing the dagger from her mouth, she jabbed the blade into his belly and twisted it as he clutched her shoulders. He fell to the deck. The stench of blood mingled with the salty scent of sea mist. She let out a rush of air and leapt over his scarlet stained corpse.

Her neck grew hot from someone gazing hard at her, she wheeled around. Anwen spotted a shadowy figure and rushed toward him. With a flick of her wrist, she pressed her dagger against the man's throat.

The full moon glowed on her catch. His hair shone like spun sunlight streaming aside a stone-smooth face adorned with striking blue-green eyes, the color of the sea. "Lugh, the sun god?"

The man gestured for her to release the blade so he could speak.

Curious as to what he had to say, she slid the sharp dagger to his chest.

He gazed straight into her eyes. "Assassin, I ask your name before you send me to the Elysian Fields."

She clutched the dagger tighter. "I am Anwen, a druid novice of Ynys Mon."

His full lips parted and he let out a sharp laugh. "The old governor slew the druids of Ynys Mon. They are all dead."

"I survived." She tilted her chin high.

"Good fortune then." He flashed a row of white teeth as

he grinned. "And now you hold a cargo of wine and fish sauce." The Roman's smile vanished and his eyes grew wide and moist. "Take it all. Just leave me my ship and crew. They are worth nothing to you."

"I think not." She took a deep breath. "Your voyage ends here." Clutching the blade hard, she flicked her wrist to stab him but her arm hung heavy. Startled and shocked, she swallowed. Jerking her head toward her crew, she yelled, "Breccan, Casnar, Torna, tie up the prisoner."

"What say you?" Starn the Stout balked at her order.

Her captive's extraordinary eyes, fathomless as the sea, drew her to him. How could a Roman be so handsome?

Thoughts swam in her head. *I do not know him. Even if I did, he's a Roman. I have to hate him.*

Laig the Dark headed scowled. "We leave no survivors, save for the Roman slaves we set free."

Wheeling toward Casnar the Valiant, she shouted, "I am in command here. Keep this one. He's my hostage." Her voice vibrated with anger for the weakness she displayed. She'd killed Romans before, many times. Why couldn't she slay him?

"How can we collect a ransom without bringing attention to ourselves?" Delbaeth asked. "Captain, you swore this would be our last raid."

The sound of bees swarmed in her brain, buzzing. Her gaze clung to the Roman's clear, vibrant eyes. She felt like rising steam, light, floating high in the air.

Turning away from him, she met the accusing and bewildered stares of her crew. "I meant slave, not hostage. Is he not a rare, precious booty, worthy of our last raid?" She turned away, ashamed of her contrived excuse.

"We free slaves." Fingen folded his arms across his barrel chest.

Anwen shook her head. "We free those enslaved to Rome but Romans can be held as slaves by Celts."

When all they gaped at her, she knew how crazy she sounded. Still, she couldn't kill the Roman. "I gave an order, get to it." She commanded, "Man the oars. Back to shore. Torna and Laig, follow with the *curragh*."

Standing at the helm as her crew rowed forward, she rested her gaze on the waves lapping at the boat. In torchlight she could make out the colors of the sea, dark to light shades of blues and greens, the hue of the Roman's eyes. On the Erinn coast, the ship docked beside the foreign vessels she'd captured long before, in previous raids.

Riona waited on the shore, six roan braids adorned with gold balls on the ends whipping about her face in the cool night breeze. She had saved Anwen from the massacre of Ynys Mon, when the Romans raided the learning center in Britannia and burned the druids alive in the oaken groves.

Riona stared, eyes wide, as two pirates dropped the Roman into her wagon. "Trussed up and hauled about like a stag tethered to a stick." Her brows arched. "Anwen, who is this?"

"I am Titus Rufius Kaeso, a merchant of Rome." The captive tilted his muscular shoulders back and lifted his firm chin.

Torna the Mystic cupped his chin. "He is her slave."

Riona rubbed her lips together as she peered at Anwen. "Did one of the Romans strike you on the head?"

"Not on the head, but the god the Romans call Cupid might have struck her with that magic arrow they speak of," Fingen the Fair quipped.

Thoughts swirled in Anwen's mind. *How can he fathom that? Do they all know?* She turned her head toward Riona.

"Don't bother making a place in your wagon for me, I will walk to the *rath*."

"Good." Riona folded her arms across her chest. "You need some fresh air."

The crew's chuckles burned Anwen's cheeks. She'd had a lack of attraction for men since she'd been attacked at Ynys Mon by the soldiers, who had left her for dead. Rage pulsed through her body even now. Every pore of her being screamed as she recalled hiding in a bog and breathing through a reed for days, until she sensed the legionnaires had left. When she climbed out of the peat bog, covered in slime, she spotted Riona. The druidess helped her into an ox hide coracle, which they rowed to Erinn. The druids of Tara offered sanctuary. There Anwen waged her own war, capturing Roman trade ships, slaughtering the crews, and freeing the slaves—until tonight.

After the legionnaires had raped her, she thought she would never desire a man the way other women did. What had changed? An image suddenly pierced her mind. All about her, in the dark, scattered around a fire, couples embraced and entwined, rocking to and fro in the rhythm of love. Her mind burned with the images and sounds. The musky scent of sex filled the air on Beltane Eve. Bare women leaped gracefully around the bonfire, their breasts bouncing up and down, as nude men with hard-muscled bodies and rigid cocks danced with them.

In this daydream, by the light of the flames, she peeled off a loose tunic dress and stood nude before her Beltane lover. He stood in all his glory adorned only with a brazen gold neck ring. Tall, with broad shoulders, his chest rippled with muscles tapering to a perfect abdomen and bulging erection. Thick and fully aroused, the length taunted her. It seemed to grow longer as she gaped at it. Her crotch coiled with tension. She burned with the need to wrap her legs around him and pull him deep into her tight passage. His eyes smoldered, flashing with a fire that entranced her. Though he could have had any woman, he wanted her, and she wanted him.

Save for thick red hair, spiking like a badger's bristles, her Beltane lover looked exactly like the Roman. She felt hot, flushed, as she recalled his arms encircling her as he crushed her against his hot, throbbing, flesh. Savagely, she dug her nails into the thick, firm muscles of his shoulders. While holding her, he buried his face against her neck and kissed the pulsating hollow at the base of her throat. Her body tingled as she recalled the sultry heat of his lips searing a path up to her mouth and hungrily covering it. The kiss created a shock wave though her entire body. He lowered her to the fertile earth. Burning for him, she arched her hips and gasped as the tip of his hard erection pressed against her tight entrance. Easing inside, he lay still within her, giving her time to stretch and adjust to the girth.

Breathless and impaled on his erection, she trembled. Pulling out completely, he drove into her in one thrust. She gasped as fire blazed through her. He rode her, sinking deep into her throbbing heat as she gazed into his eyes. Her heart pounded as she recalled this had been more than coupling around the towering Beltane blaze for fertility rites—she loved him. They burned for each other, entwined as one. Fire seemed to swallow them whole, their passion feeding the inferno. As memories flooded her mind, she felt her hot, moist *fagina* tighten. Her breath quickened.

She recalled that he'd gazed in her eyes and said, "We shall wed at Lughnasa."

As joy filled her, she remembered answering him excitedly, "Yes, we shall marry come the Lughnasa feast."

Her body jerked, startled. She shook her mind free of the strange musings. How could she have loved this Roman, Kaeso, in a previous life?

Another thought pierced her mind. *This has to be the work of that trickster sea god, Mannon.* Anwen met the druidess' gaze. "I'm going to the sacred copse on the hill instead."

"To pray to the gods?" Riona's eyes grew wide and sad, she cupped her chin. "Now?"

"Yes, I need perform a ritual to Mannon Mac Lir." Anwen stomped off toward the narrow path and up the green hill. "The sea god and I need to talk."

AFTER STOPPING along the dirt path to gather two generous handfuls of lush, green grass, she entered the copse of ancient oaks. Clutching a bundle of grass in each hand, she faced the oldest, gnarled oak. Ancient wisdom vibrated from the tree, energizing her. Like branches reaching for the sky, she stretched her arms high.

She shook her fists full of green grass, chanting, "I invoke your name, Mannon, Mannon, Mannon Mac Lir. I summon you to me. Mighty magician, son of the sea, Mannon appear." Anwen leaped to the rhythm of her chant. Clicking heel to shin, she danced in a circle before the oak, shaking the blades of grass. "Mannon Mac Lir, heed my call, take your offering." Dancing feverishly, she twirled around as the wind lifted her hair. "Mannon Mac Lir, as I give to you, give to me." She opened up her fist and laughed in rapt happiness, spinning faster and faster as the wind tossed the green blades high in the air and blew them out to sea for the god. "Bless you for accepting my meager offering, Son of the Sea." Anwen chanted, "Mighty magician, you brought a man to me."

The howling wind, the god's voice whistled the words, "You mortals think we do all for you."

"Do you say you did not bring him?" Her skin pickled as a cold chill coursed through her.

"You summoned him. By craving a past lover, you called him forth to be born again."

"What?" Dizziness overcame her. "No." She shut her eyes and tried to still her spinning thoughts. "I could not have loved the Roman in another life?"

"Why do you keep calling him Roman?"

Her eyes flew open. "He is."

The wind whispered, "He is Roman in this life only."

She rubbed her forehead. "It cannot be."

"Yet, it is so."

A chill ran up her spine as the eerie breathy wind continued to speak for the god.

"Though neither of you knew it, he traveled across the dangerous sea to find you. And you, Anwen, began raiding Roman ships for the chance to meet him."

"No." Anwen didn't like the shakiness in her voice, but this revelation shook her to the core.

"Yes. You sought him out and here he is. Be happy."

The wind stilled. An overpowering hush filled the air. The god had accepted her offering, shared his wisdom and had now departed.

"In another time, the Roman and I swore to be together again, in a new life." Anwen hung her head. "This life."

TWO

Focusing on the shadowy shapes surrounding him, Kaeso's eyes adjusted to the dark. He found himself held in this dreary *southerrain*, as they called it, after two pirates shoved him down a ladder. Then after yanking up the rickety ladder, they'd shut the hatch.

"By Mars. A female pirate from Ynys Mon," he said to himself. Flame red hair, eyes of emerald shards, and a face as fair as Venus', filled his mind. His thoughts turned to her breasts jutting beneath that drab, mannish tunic and her ample hips and plush rear straining against her unbecoming braies.

He pounded his fist on the table in front of him. If he hadn't gawked, moon mad at her, captured her gaze, he could have slayed both those men and escaped. Kicking over the table, it crashed to the floor with a bang. His foot throbbed with pain. He failed the crew of his merchant ship. Now he was but a plump pig on the priest's sacrificial block.

Think, think! The captain and her men were arguing. I can use that, along with her attraction to me, to my advan-

tage. She did seem to like me. Oh, I cannot think of that now. Those are the type of thoughts that got me here.

The windowless chamber reeked of a musky odor, yet he could smell the aromatic scent of fresh baked bread from above. *So, I'm below the hearth. Well, if I do escape, I know where the hatch leads to.* As he scanned the room, he gasped when his gaze fell on a human skull peering down from the top of a crude cupboard. It reminded him of savage Celts hanging severed heads from their horse's necks as tokens of battle.

Kaeso turned away and tried to concentrate on escape, but a sensation of falling overcame him. He snapped his neck back. Again, he'd faded out, like nodding off to sleep but faster, harder...more intense. He shook his head as his mind spun with the image of Anwen's sculptured face and the six braids streaming to the hem of her short, black tunic that clung to every curve of her body. As he remembered those shapely thighs incased in black braies, his arousal stirred. He'd never wanted a woman the way he did her. Kaeso sensed he knew her...loved her. Madness. Had she cast a spell, some type of druid enchantment, on him?

The creaking sound and flicker of light revealed that someone had opened the hatch. The ladder was lowered and a figure with long legs, garbed in black braies, descended the rickety rungs.

"Captain, I am honored by your presence," he said hoarsely. His mind burned with the thought of tugging her braies down her ample hips and thighs, to spread those long legs and feel the hot flesh of them wrapped around his hips. "It is unbearably hot in here." A fever overtook him as he imagined prodding her moist, tight opening. Sinking into it. Deep.

Her russet eyebrows arched in bafflement. "I'm not hot. It's damp and cool in the *southerrain*."

The air brimmed with the tempting scents of shellfish, salmon and heady drink. He noticed the tray she clutched, of oysters and clams, a large honey-coated fish, and a brass horn filled with golden mead.

"I brought food." Anwen glanced at the overturned table, then waited for him to right it before setting the meal down. She picked up a clam with her slender fingers. As she pressed it against her full lips, they formed a perfect circle.

A surge of heat shot through him and he stiffened as she sucked the soft flesh deep into her mouth. He steeled his expression into one of anger at his foe. "You cannot charm me with your druid spell of enchantment." He lied. He wanted nothing more at that moment than to bend her over the surface of the table, rip her braies off, and burry his hard erection in the sweet fire nestled between her creamy thighs.

"No one is trying to charm you." She caught him gaping at her and chided, "Tarry not over your dinner, Roman, or I will feed it to the dogs."

He knew she didn't try to entrance him, though her shapely body emitted as much sexual heat as a bevy of young, nude pleasure slaves. And all this Celtic pirate had to do, to raise the fire of lust in him, was climb down a rickety ladder or suck a shellfish. Needing to sate his hunger somehow, he grabbed a chunk of salmon and sank his teeth into it. The heady but appetizing taste wrapped around his tongue. He took bite after bite, chewing eagerly, then wiped his chin with the back of his hand.

With his stomach appeased, he found it easier to think on a more pressing matter than the shrew's body. "Lady, as your prisoner, I request you give me the date of my execution...or sacrifice."

Her eyes widened in shock and her face grew pale.

Again, he snapped his neck back. He blacked out for a moment, though no longer than the blink of an eye. His mind found the word sacrifice too disturbing, anytime he said, heard or thought it, he had a traumatic response.

He watched her body jerk as his had. Then he picked up the brass horn, taking a long gulp of thick, golden mead as he thought, *It can't be. It makes no sense.*

Stepping back, she shifted her gaze away from him as if to get her bearings. "I'm not going to kill you and no one would dare harm you while under my protection. Bards sing paeans of my sword skill in all five kingdoms of Erinn. At one time, god kings were sacrificed, but no longer." She gulped. "You are a Roman and would not be a god king anyway. Only the best warrior—the champion of the Lughnasa games—was chosen. But it is an old custom, no longer followed."

He set the brass horn down on the table with a clank and wondered why a druidess from Ynys Mon would protect him. Yet when he gazed into her eyes, he was certain he knew her and trusted her with his life. A flutter of warmth flowed through him. He felt close to her, as if she'd always been by his side. As if she knew him better than anyone.

"M'lady, you spared my life. How shall I reward such valiant service?"

"I ask no reward of you."

He stepped closer. "My ship?" His gaze fell onto her plump pink lips. "My cargo?" He watched, breathless, as they parted slightly. "Ah, lady I shall offer you my kiss." He licked his lips.

Her throat bobbed as she swallowed.

Kaeso took her face in his hands. His fingers quivered. His palms melted into the softness and warmth of her skin. His breath caught in his throat as he leaned forward. Their lips met. The sensation of licking flames overcame him. He crushed his lips against the hot, wet flesh of hers. Smothering her mouth, he sucked its sweetness. Then, parting her lips with his tongue, he thrust it into her mouth. The sensual sounds of her moans boiled his blood. These were the lips he remembered, the taste, the softness of them. The warm, full lips he had searched forever since he began turning his head to take a second glance at maidens walking down the streets of Rome.

He tore his mouth away from Anwen's swollen lips. His heart raced. A vivid daydream of flames stirred in his mind, a blazing bonfire dancing before him. So real. And she was there. At his side. Three daisies embellished her flame red hair, which fell loose, unbraided. A chain of spring flowers, with white petals and bright yellow centers, dangled from her slender neck to her jutting, pink-tipped breasts. Her gleaming eyes, full of hunger, impaled him. She stood nude before him except for a symbol of the sun painted on her shoulder in woad.

Moans and panting sounded from all the Beltane partners making love before the hot fire. But he had eyes only for her. His mind filled with unbidden memories. A man stood near them, wearing the full antler headdress of the hunter god Cerrenous. He was the god king, the champion of all warriors, winner of the Lughnasa games and treated as a king for one year. All the women wanted him. Three stood with him now, all young and beautiful, sharing him. The god king's body glistened with sweat by the light of the bonfire. One of the women took off the man's antler headdress as the other two took him by his hands, and with their guidance, he sank to the ground. All four moved together in a fierce frenzy of passion. Though his body burned with need, Kaeso hadn't envied the god king. He only wanted the woman who stood before him. Only her.

His body jerked as a woman's voice interrupted his vivid memories. "Answer me, Roman. Are you all right?"

Anwen's query drew him from his musings. He opened his mouth to answer the lady captain, but the hard knot in his throat caused him to pause. The woman in his daydream looked the same as her.

"You fell into a trance. Are you well?"

"Well?" He absently scratched his head then dropped his arm to his side. "No." He felt strange, dizzy and confused. "Tell me, what is a god king?"

"In days of old, a man was chosen for the greatest honor. After a year, treated as a king, all his desires met, he went to the gods and pleaded for his tribe so the crops would not fail and the cattle would grow fat and healthy. His sacrifice insured the tribe's survival."

"You mean, at his death, when the druid killed him, he went to the gods?"

"There is no greater honor, but the custom is no longer followed." Anwen rose. "Roman, you need to eat. I will come back for the tray." She turned, climbed up the rungs of the ladder to the top floor, and slammed the hatch.

Kaeso stared at the stone wall. His knees grew weak and he crumpled into the wooden chair. A sharp pain pierced his head. "God king." Why did the words make him tremble?

ANWEN DRAPED a plaid cloak over her shoulders and pinned it to her tunic with a round broach. With her mind in a daze,she wandered outside. Aimlessly, she strolled past grazing cattle to the rock-strewn shore, barely feeling hard stones press against the soles of her feet. She came to a standstill upon the wet sand. Her bare toes crushed the pliant white grains as the tide rushed against her tingling feet. She flung back her head, yanking one braid at a time to unravel her mane.

The wind ruffled her hair as it fell to her thighs. When the Roman had said god king, a vision sprung in her mind of him nude, before a crowd, a garrote around his neck. A druid had twisted it and the man dropped dead.

She'd screamed out, "I love you." Her heart pounded. Anwen stretched her arms up to the pink and blue sunset and prayed. "Mannon, son of the sea, save my heart. Whatever took place in the past this man is my enemy now. I know we were robbed of a life together before, but I cannot love a Roman. Help me harden my heart against him. For this cannot be."

She unfastened the broach, slipped off her cloak, shucked off her tunic and braies, and strode waist-deep into the cool, briny water. As she floated, letting the waves roll her out to sea, the knots in her muscles unraveled and happy thoughts of Kaeso filled her mind. The height of his muscular body, the tingling warmth of his rock hard biceps crushing her against the solid wall of his bare chest... and his kiss.

The moment their lips had touched, glowing warmth had swirled through her. She'd felt complete, as if she'd found a part of herself that had been lost. She knew she'd kissed him many times before. No one's lips felt or tasted like his, warm, salty, and fresh. The flavor of his mouth and the male musk of his scent held all the beauty and danger of the sea in a storm. She couldn't forget the sensations of his essence in a million lifetimes.

After the swim, Anwen spread her plaid cloak on the soft sand and slept there. As she drifted to sleep, the sea breeze played with her hair and swept down her body like the touch of human hands—his hands—making her tingle. In her dream, Kaeso's firm palms and breath stroked her face and sent warm shivers through her body. A deep moan escaped her lips as she imagined him pressing the soft flesh of her breasts, mashing them, one in each of his large hands. Her flesh burned as he squeezed the swelling peaks and spirals of heat swirled through her. His hot lips swooped down and kissed her nipple, tongue whisking and teeth nudging against it. Passion throbbed through her as she fantasized.

His probing hands moved downward, skimming both sides of her body all the way to her thighs. Craving contact with his flesh, she arched, seeking to meld into him, to burn together in one blaze. She gasped as his hardened erection pressed against her moist entrance. She spread her legs, instinctively, offering up her body for his taking. The hardness of his muscled thigh brushed against her tingling flesh as he straddled her. She gazed into his eyes and then glanced at the stars above.

Her memories were so clear. After they'd picked bilberries until the dark of night, as was the custom on Lughnasa, they coupled together. Baskets of bilberries lay scattered over the hill as the couples who picked them lay entwined, panting, moaning and moving together in a rocking motion. His palms pressed against her thighs to spread them wider, and she thrust her hips forward to meet him. His rock hard cock slid into her. She quivered. The walls of her sex stretched as he sunk deeper into her. So slowly, her hunger peaked, and she let out a mewl of need. Whimpering with desire, she welcomed his hard thrust. Though he was so large, she had to take him. She had to have him. She held nothing back. Her mind delved further into the fantasy.

With a thrust of her hips, she drew him in deeper. She strained against the girth and length of him, raising her knees as he began to move upon her with slithering strokes. He pulled out of her and paused for one moment then lunged into her depths. She gasped and shrieked.

Arching to meet his thrust, her pulse pounded and her breath rushed in and out in shallow pants. She writhed as he hammered her into a frenzy. On the brink of release, she moaned as he thrashed wildly. A rush of maddening sensations seized her as she clenched around him. He groaned and burst inside her. In the blinding, pulsing moment, she cried out in climax with uninhibited pleasure. Their hot juices flowed together like molten lava.

Her eyes flew open, awakened by her own scream. She was alone. On the sand. Her heart hammered. It was all so real, her pussy coiled tight, throbbing with need. She panted just like in the dream as moisture pooled between her legs. Her body throbbed and ached for him. Anwen fought to steel her passion. They had been together, a thousand years ago, but her body still recalled the feel of him inside her.

She rasped aloud, "Gods help me."

Desires she thought had died with her friends at Ynys Mon had been awaken by this lover from a previous life. She didn't care at that moment that he was Roman. He was hers and she was his. The blazing, amber sun rose over the sea, streaming lemon, corral, and burnt orange ribbons across the sky. It was morning, she had slept all night.

Anwen pulled her brat up off the sand and folded it into the shape of a large pouch. She walked along the soft sand collecting seaweed. At least it would look like she'd done something that morning. She had to get back to the *rath*. If not, her men and, worse, Riona, would come looking for her soon. Sand clung to her clothes as she strode home, clutching her cloak, folded like a bag and laden with freshly gathered seaweed. She didn't want to face her men or Riona. If they asked where she had been, what would she tell them?

As soon as she reached out to open the door, a figure stepped forward, startling her for a moment. "Starn, good morn."

"Captain, if the Roman needs food or anything, I or one of the other men can bring it to him," he said in a deep, gruff voice. "We all know what you suffered at the hands of the Romans. There is no need for you to be alone with one of them."

She took a deep breath and managed a smile. "My thanks, Starn. I am not afraid of the Roman or any man."

He didn't move out of the way, so she had to squeeze past him. As she entered the stone round house, all her other men inside breaking their fast turned their eyes upon her. "Good morn, all."

"I heard the murmurs about a lump of sand serving as your bed last eve." Riona tilted her head toward Anwen.

"I do not wish to speak about it. I have much on my mind." She laid her cloak on the table to show Riona. "I gathered seaweed for us this morning."

She had always been able to talk to the druidess, but she couldn't speak of her feelings for the Roman. Questions kept turning over in her mind, wondering how he felt about her, if he remembered her, if he knew he'd been a hero—a god king. He gave his life to travel to the Otherworld and plead for their tribe. And the crops were fruitful the next year. She gasped. He had asked what a god king was. He remembered. She let out a deep sigh. He died for the whole tribe, and then he came back in this life. He'd returned for her.

She glanced at the seaweed and tossed it into a copper cauldron filled with boiling water. Riona stirred a cup of goat's milk into the cauldron, creating a delicious pot of *carrageen*. Anwen scooped the brew onto an earthen platter, added a bowl of honeyed oat porridge, and a loaf of fresh bread from the clay-domed oven. She strolled to the hatch with platter in hand.

"Captain," Starn called out.

She turned toward him and the rest of her crew. "I need to speak to the hostage, men. All is well."

She opened the small hatch door. Her heart beat erratically.

THREE

At the squeak of the door hatch, the aroma of oats and fresh baked bread wafted through the air. Kaeso rubbed his lips together as Anwen climbed down the ladder. He watched her lush rear, wiggling in the tight Celtic braies. Then, he feasted his eyes on her long, graceful legs as they moved down the crude rungs. He noticed something different about her. Her movements were stiff as if she was tense and her legs shook. If she wasn't careful her foot might slip.

He rushed forward holding his arms out and caught her just as she fell. The tray crashed to the ground. With a loud bang the clay jug shattered into pieces. As its contents formed a puddle on the floor, the heady smell of ale filled the room.

Her breath grew shallow, heaving from the shock of falling. Without thought, his gaze rested on the rise and fall of her breasts, then shifted to her face. Her full lips parted as she sucked in sharp breaths. He heard his own breath rushing fast and hard. A blast of inner heat hit him. The stirring in his balls intensified, drawing tight as if squeezed hard. The curve of her breast molded to his chest as he snugly cradled her in his arms. His gaze met hers. Her startled expression softened into a half-lidded, enthralling look.

Before he knew it, his mouth covered hers. He pressed his lips hard against hers. His lips tingled as they clung to hers. He dragged and twisted his mouth over hers. Anwen's lips were so warm and sweet. Kaeso let out a low moan.

Someone with a gruff voice interrupted them, asking, "What is this?"

Kaeso hadn't even noticed the hatch had been opened. He broke the kiss and snapped his head toward the man who stood on the ladder.

Anwen shoved her hands against Kaeso's chest. "Put me down, Roman."

He set her on her feet but didn't tear his gaze from her. Anwen's lips were still wet and swollen, and even though she spoke to him now like she hated him, it didn't lessen his burning need to kiss her again.

She slid her feet into a warrior stance, lifted her chin, and addressed the man called Starn. "I slipped on the ladder. The Roman caught me."

"Slipped?" Starn girpped the side of the ladder, but didn't move his feet off of the middle rung.

"That is true." Anwen set one hand on her hip. "So beware of the ladder yourself. One of the rungs must be loose."

Starn's eyes narrowed as the muscles in his face tensed. "Someone should pick up this mess." He swept his gaze across the spilled ale and scattered food on the floor. "They're rats down here. As you know...Captain." He turned his head away and scurried up the ladder.

Before Kaeso could say a word to comfort Anwen, the woman he saw earlier peered down from the opened hatch. "What happened?"

Anwen let the arm on her hip fall to her side "Riona." She scrubbed her forehead. "I dropped the tray. Bring more food for the Roman."

Riona leaned her head further into the open hatch. "Did the ladder break?"

Anwen set both hands on her hips. "The hostage must be fed." She took a deep breath and softened her tone as she said, "Please, I ask of you, bring a tray of food."

"As you wish." Riona moved away from the hatch.

Kaeso stepped toward Anwen.

She jerked her hands up, palms out. "Do not touch me."

"And why not, when you desire my touch so much?"

"We are enemies. No matter how much I may think I know you or knew you, I don't. The thoughts in my head are madness. I hate Romans. Nothing will change that." Anwen's thin eyebrows slanted downward. "Nothing."

"So, you've been thinking of me." He knew she didn't hate him. Far from it. No matter what she said. "I'm curious, what do you mean, no matter how much I think I know you or knew you?"

Anwen leaned her head back as she peered at him. "Why did you ask me about the god kings?"

"Why do you ask now?" Flakes of sand glistened upon her smooth skin. She smelled of salt and seaweed. An image flashed in his mind of stretching out nude on the sand as the tide ebbed and flowed beside him. With Anwen on top of him, his arms wrapped around the slender waist of her bare, wet body. Bracing her as she set on his cock and rode him. Her round breasts bouncing as he pumped her deeper, faster, while wave after wave of pleasure rolled through him.

"You've been to the shore this morn." His erection hardened and throbbed.

Before Anwen could answer a female voice interrupted her. "Here's the food."

He jerked his head toward Riona who stood on the ladder, gazing at Anwen. "Come get it. I don't want to climb any further and hit that bad rung you told Starn about."

He couldn't help but notice her sarcastic tone and he was sure Anwen didn't miss it either.

Anwen walked over to the ladder, lifted her arms and took the tray. "Starn talks too much."

Riona snorted as she gazed intensely at Anwen. "We'll talk later." She turned and climbed back up the ladder. With a loud bang she slammed the hatch.

Anwen set the tray down on the small oaken table. "Here's your food, unspilled this time."

"Captain, will you break your fast with me?"

"Why not?" Anwen dropped into the chair at the table, facing him.

Grabbing the clay pitcher of ale, he poured them both a cup. "Why did you spend the night at the shore?"

Taking the cup from him, she took a generous swig. "I needed to get away."

"You could have taken me with you." Holding the cup to his mouth, he drained the last drop of ale.

She shrugged. "I could never go away with a Roman."

Kaeso picked up a piece of flat bread and dipped it into the mix of milk and seaweed and then took a generous bite. "What do you plan to do with me?"

"I should have killed you, but I couldn't do it. So I'll release you. I don't take hostages or slaves." Anwen grabbed the bowl of porridge and dipped her spoon into the white gruel. "We feast tonight to celebrate our last raid." She slid the spoon between her lips, ate the porridge and ran her tongue across her upper lip. "I will free you then."

He imagined her lips stretched around his erect shaft rather than the spoon. "Free me?"

"I'll keep your ship. You can row a *coracle* to Londinium." She scooped up another glob of porridge and sucked if off the spoon.

"Your men will not object?" He grabbed the other spoon and scooped up a wad of *carrageen.*

"No one knows you're here, save my crew, and they want you to leave." She picked up a piece of warm bread. "Besides, I'm the captain, they do as I say. And I think it's best you get far away from me, soon."

He chewed the sticky vegetable, which had a mild taste of seawater. "Why, do you not like me?" He grinned.

"You make me think too much." She bit into the hunk of bread. When she finished chewing, she asked, "Have you had thoughts of me?"

"Yes." *Mad ones. Right now. You make me crazy.* "You killed my men and took me prisoner. I think of you often." He fought to hide the passion pulsating through his body, the frantic beat of his heart, the ache in his groin. "Why not release me now?"

"It's best to free you at the feast."

One moment he was thinking, *Come with me,* then realized he said it aloud.

"Go with you?" She sat back, grabbed a strand of her hair, and twisted it around her finger, fidgeting. "I am a druidess of the learning center."

He spotted the glimmer of a tear in her eye.

"Your people set the sacred oaks on fire and threw my friends into the flames." Her voice tightened as if she was in pain. "The druids of Tara offered me safe haven." She pulled her fingers out of her hair and ran her hand down her throat, then crossed her arms. "You're a Roman, I'm a Celt."

She stood and turned her back to him. Her grief ripped through him. He knew then that his heart had sought this woman across the seven seas. He hadn't become a merchant to seek riches—he'd done it to find her.

Kaeso heard a faint sob as Anwen climbed the ladder. When she shut the hatch, his small dungeon seemed unbearably empty. He missed her already. His voice seemed to boom through the quiet, dark basement, "We were not always Roman and Celt. I don't know how, but we were together once...and far from enemies."

ANWEN'S HEART was like a dried out well. Whoever the man Kaeso had been before had died for her and the tribe. Now that he had returned she had to look upon him as dead to her, because he'd come back as a Roman.

Wandering to the back of the round house, she sought Riona at her loom.

"My thanks for the food." Her eyes followed Riona's long, slender fingers hanging thin warp threads and tying on tiny weights. Pulling to and fro, Riona twisted and turned flimsy threads into strong woolen cloth.

Riona smiled. "As you said, the hostage has to eat." She pointed her head toward three baskets of dyed wool. "Remember when we brewed the colors, blue for the Erinn Sea, black for eternity, and green for growth? Finally, I have the time to work with them. I must make haste to finish the task before the cold wind blows." Riona's fingers and wrist danced as she wove. "This weave will make fine winter cloaks." When Anwen didn't respond, Riona's twinkling eyes seemed to dim. "You must release the Roman. He has enchanted you."

Anwen scraped her front teeth across her lower lip. "Yes, this eve, at the feast I will grant him his freedom."

"Will you leave with him?" Riona's eyebrows arched.

"What say you? He's a Roman."

Riona shook her head. "I saw the way you looked at him and he at you. You might have been lovers in a previous life."

Startled, Anwen gasped. "How did you know? Yes, it is so. Mannon Mac Lir revealed it and...I have memories."

Riona pulled her fingers off the loom and settled them in her lap. "Love is never simple, but you cannot fight it. This Roman may be your destiny."

Anwen felt like she'd been turned upside down. "Then I will not fulfill my destiny. I cannot."

Riona returned her fingers to the loom. Steadily, turning the spindle with her thumb as her upturned fingers shaped the threads. "Where will the Roman go?"

Anwen drew in a deep breath. "Londinium, where he was headed."

Riona pulled the threads with her right hand, smoothing them out with her left. As Anwen watched, the thought, *smooth me out,* pierced her mind. If only your nimble fingers could gather my unraveling thoughts and weave them into one strong strand once more. "I must let him go."

Riona stood, and took Anwen into her loving arms. "I don't think it's up to you."

Anwen laid her head on her friend's warm shoulder, drawing in the strength and comfort of friendship. "What do you mean?"

Before the druidess could answer a sudden noise drew Anwen's attention.

She swung her head toward the sound. She spotted

Starn snooping on her conversation. He turned his back to her and strode away in a fast gait.

Why would Starn act like that? Where was he going? A sense of dread filed her. She pulled away from Riona. "Did he hear me? What will he do?"

She barely heard Riona's words, "It's up to the gods."

Anwen had no time to think about the druidess' advice, she dashed outside. Her heart hammered as she glimpsed Starn vaulting onto a shaggy, roan pony and galloping at a dirt-kicking pace toward the druid center of Tara. She was too late to stop him.

She rubbed her lips together, thinking he must have simply chosen to leave her crew since he didn't approve of her decision to keep the Roman alive. She had too much on her mind to worry about Starn.

FOUR

Kaeso felt a warm flutter in his chest as he gazed at Anwen's face while she leaned into the open hatch. He clung to the side of the ladder as he climbed toward her. The sunny sensation changed to a chill as he realized he was headed to the worst day of his life. Anwen would free him today. Send him away. He'd spend the rest of his life thinking about her. Longing for her.

He stepped off the ladder and, with an appreciative glance at the curve of her ass in her tight braies, he followed Anwen into a large, round room. She gracefully lowered herself onto a thick fur pelt on the floor and crossed her legs in a seated position. He sat on a deer pelt across from her. A servant handed him a clay plate with a boiled boar leg on it.

As he clutched his dinner, he raked his eyes over the length of her bright plaid gown. His gaze lingered on the curves of her well-proportioned breasts and hips. He shifted his gaze to her eyes, wide pools of sensuous light. A savage inner fire flared in his erection, hardening it. Kaeso couldn't leave her. He had to have her. If only he could stay in her *southerrain*. He'd at least get to see her each day when she brought his food. With that thought, he grabbed the boar leg and gnawed on the juicy meat.

Raising up on her knees, she crawled toward him. Dropping the boar leg onto the plate, he then set the whole thing on the floor at his side.

Anwen curled her soft fingers around his forearm and leaned her head to his. Her breath blew hot against his flesh.

His ear tingled as she whispered, "Dance with me, Roman."

His heart thudded. "I know not the Celtic steps." He wanted to move with her. Over and under her, but dancing wasn't what he had in mind.

"I'll teach you." She stood, grabbed his hands, and tugged him up and toward the hearth. "It is a grand floor for dancing, laid with fresh rushes."

Heat coursed through his body from the mere touch of her hands on his. He gulped. "Will this be one of the dances I have heard druids do nude in the moonlight?"

"Roman," she chided, "keep your clothes on."

"I feared we would have to stay fully dressed." His skin felt so hot from her nearness, he wanted to rip his clothes off, but only after he tore hers off first.

Placing the wooden fife between her lips, Riona played a merry tune at a fast-paced rhythm.

Kaeso awkwardly jumped and kicked to the beat, trying to match Anwen's high steps and graceful leaps. Stumbling into a near fall, he laughed. "I cannot do it."

Her flushed face spurred thoughts of him holding her in his arms through the night, plunging deep into her, thrusting in and out, until he burst inside her and she screamed with pleasure, as she had many times with him, so many years ago.

"It's good." The even whiteness of her lively smile was dazzling. "We have danced all the way to the door."

"I am getting a feel for it." He offered her a wide grin and warm laugh.

With the trembling of her lips, the smile vanished, and her expressive face sobered. "Come."

With slow, heavy steps she led him outside. He followed her down to the beach, where sand merged with white-capped waves. She pointed to a *coracle* beached on the shore.

In a strained, faint tone Anwen said, "It is time to leave."

KAESO'S GAZE locked with hers. Leave? He never wanted to leave her again. He reached out and cupped her face. He swallowed tightly. "Lady, let us dance upon the sand."

"There's no fife or harp to carp a tune," she said in a silky whisper.

"I shall sing to you, Ovid's poem, Amores." In a tone muted with lust he recited, "'Hair parted along her ivory neck.'"Lifting one hand, he brushed his fingertips down her graceful neck in feathery strokes. Her skin was so warm and smooth. Moving his hand to her face, he traced the outline of her lips. Tenderly, he covered her mouth with his.

As he rolled his fingertips down the silky skin of her right arm, he rested his other hand on her waist, pulling her against him. She slid her arms around his neck. Bodies pressed together, their feet moving in small rhythmic steps, they glided across the sand. Dancing to the roar of rushing, white-foamed waves. He eased his lips off hers. The smoldering depths of her eyes entranced him. He reeled from the rush of desire for her.

Bending at the knee, he slid down her body and gathered up the hem of her tunic-dress, drawing it up her legs, hips, waist, breasts, and over her head. Tossing the garment on the sand, he quoted another line of Amores. "'Such graceful arms I saw and touched.'" His fingers danced down her soft skin. Pressing his lips to her palm, he planted butterfly kisses from her wrist to the shallow at her elbow, and all the way to the sensuous curve of her shoulder. Kaeso's desire built as he whispered the poet's words, "'How sweet her breast ready for an embrace.'" Then he cupped her swan white bust and stroked the thrusting peaks. Palming one, he brushed his lips against the other erect nipple.

She mewed with delight.

In a serpentine stroke, he slid his palm to her stomach. While nudging her navel with the tip of his finger and rolling it in a slow circular motion, he rasped Ovid's words. "'What a smooth belly.'" Sliding his palm over her tummy, he moved the heel of his hand in gentle, circular strokes. In a deep, ragged tone he quoted another line. "'I pressed her naked body to my own.'" He crushed her to his chest and smothered her mouth with his.

Anwen let out a deep moan.

He broke the kiss to suck in a quick breath of air. He gazed at her flushed face. "Ovid's lover could not match your beauty. Might you be the muse that gifted him with Amores?"

Peeling off his tunic, he threw it to the wind. He drank in the perfection of her up-tilted breasts and curved hips. His hands ached to touch her, to feel her hot, smooth flesh against his. Blood rushed to his cock as fiery heat coursed through his body.

He swung her into the circle of his arms. With a fierce hunger he reclaimed her slick, soft lips.

As he pressed his mouth against hers, he eased her down onto the sand. Gliding one hand across her flat stomach to the swell of her hips, fire tore through him. His balls and cock pulsed with pressure, his need for her was so great. It made no difference that she was a Celt and he a Roman. All that mattered was that they had each other right now.

Slipping his hand to the apex of her thighs, he moaned as she arched her back and spread her legs, opening fully to him. He peered between her creamy thighs, into her tight depth. He brushed one finger down the center of her pussy. Unfolding the pink petals with his fingers, he gazed intensely at them as he dipped a long finger into her wet heat. He dragged his finger back and forth. Teasing her. His breath grew shallow and his heart raced.

He thrust two fingers into her sheath. Anwen gasped. Hot and wet, her pussy clenched his fingers. His head spun from the musky scent of her arousal. Kaeso probed deeper into her slick passage. He rocked his fingers inside her in a gentle rhythm. Then rapidly, he whisked her throbbing flesh.

Driven to a frenzy of pleasure, her lips curved to a perfect circle as she sucked in sharp breaths. He slid in a third finger, stretching her tight passage. She grew wetter from his strokes. His arousal stiffened, burned, and pained for her.

He locked his gaze with Anwen. His voice came rough and hoarse as he asked, "Do you want me to replace my fingers with my cock?"

In a breathy voice, strained with lust she rasped, "Yes."

Unable to hold back a moment more, he straddled her thighs, rubbing the head of his erection against her slick folds and prodding her tight entrance. Sliding slowly into her, he drew back, and then in one fast, deep thrust, he speared her, forcing air from her lungs. Filled with an intoxicated rush, he moved on her. No other woman felt like Anwen. So hot. So tight. So right.

Their bodies rocked to a primeval rhythm. She raised her legs, wrapping them around his shoulders. He pushed higher, harder. Anwen's body melded to him. Pleasure flooded him. His gaze fell on her pink-tipped breasts, heaving with his thrusts. He slid his hands up to the beautifully formed mounds, cupping the soft flesh. He squeezed her breasts. He nudged the erect rosy tips with his fingers.

A moan escaped from deep within her. Anwen's eyes were hooded and glassy with desire. Her breathing fell into rapid huffs.

He grasped her hips. Each time he slammed into her moist heat, it felt as hot and wet as dipping into liquid fire. Digging his fingertips into her soft flesh, he ground into her pussy. He let out feral groans as her inner muscles gripped and squeezed him. Anwen bucked beneath him as he drove in and out, pounding her pussy. Shuddering in a frenzied spasm, she came hard and fast.

Moaning in blissful agony, he arched and cried out, "Anwen." He burst, flooding into her. His molten release mingled with hers.

Her lips parted as if she was speaking to him, but her words were drowned out by the thunderous gallop of war horses. He glanced toward the sound to see that each steed was mounted by a spiral helmeted warrior brandishing a long spear. He pulled out of Anwen, eased his body off hers and jerked to his feet. Before he could fight or flee, the men fell upon him.

With tears flowing down her face, Anwen stood. She grabbed her tunic-dress off the sand and yanked it over her head, briskly slipping her arms through the sleeves then tugging it down her body.

"Let him go."Anwen shook her fists.

A tall man, with long red hair and a thick moustache bellowed, "By commandment of the king, we take him to the druid. This Roman will be sacrificed."

"No." Anwen rushed the warriors, pounding their backs with her fists, but they pushed her down, onto to the sand. She rose to her feet and pointed to Kaeso's clothes strewn on the sand. She grabbed Kaeso's long Roman tunic and shoved it into a spearman's arms. "Let him dress."

Kaeso briskly tugged his clothes on, glad the warriors offered him some dignity, though he knew they were here to take him to his death. Suddenly, he was overcome with the sensation that this had happened before. Sacrifice. An image focused in his mind. He quivered with the depth and intensity of the vivid memory. His soul had risen from his body, still collared at the neck by the garrote the druid had twisted to squeeze the life out of him. As he waited for Goddess Arianrhod to sail through the sky on her ship, Oar Wheel, and carry him to the Otherworld to await his rebirth, he tried to think of some way to stay. He recalled the reason he didn't want go to the utopia of the forever summer of the Otherworld. He couldn't bear to leave his woman.

Tears had drenched her face as she'd screamed with pain at his death. He vowed he'd return to her in the next life. Though she had a different name, she and Anwen were the same soul. He loved her then and he loved her no less now.

He shifted his gaze to Anwen. His heart lurched at her tears. "I've been here before. I've crushed your soft lips to mine and burned as our flesh pressed together. As we joined as one, I fell in love with your soul. That is why I had to come back. If I must be sacrificed again, just to have a few moments with you...then so be it."

"I say no." Anwen's tone was soft but firm. "I will not be robbed of our love a second time." She impaled him with her fierce gaze.

Briskly, the king's men tied his hands and hauled him onto a foaming roan pony. Anwen was no longer in his line of vision. He yelled out, "Lady, I love you. I shall love you for all time."

A warrior leapt onto the horse and grasped Kaeso's waist with one hand as he clutched the reigns with the other. Before Kaeso could hear Anwen's reply or steal one last glance of her, the last chance he had to see her in this life, the Celtic pony carried him off at a hard gallop.

FIVE

Anwen dropped to her knees in the sand. She watched the last of the horses kick up the white grains along the shoreline as the war band galloped away with the man she loved. "They can't kill him. They took him from me once, but never again."

A memory arose from the depths of her soul. Kaeso, a little different, with red hair, yet eyes of the same vivid blue, with a gold torque banding his neck and a plaid cloak draping his shoulders, stood beside her, within the wooden walls of a hill fort. She clutched his hands as a druid approached.

The thin man with weather-worn skin, wearing a cloak of crow feathers, told him, "Now, God King, it is time for your journey to the otherworld."

The redheaded Kaeso spoke of having waited a year for the honor. Having won the games at the Lughnasa feast the year before, he held the title, God King. Now, a year later at Lughnasa, he would be sacrificed. His spirit would sail to the gods and plea for a plentiful crop next year so the tribe wouldn't starve.

She remembered crying as the druid took him to the harvest mound, symbolizing earth clumped over a seed to germinate. Shuddering violently, she relived the moment the druid fastened a garrote around her lover's neck. Sobbing, she rocked back and forth, her insides squeezing in pain. The priest turned the stick. He—her man—this earlier Kaeso slumped down. Her heart ripped. She flung her hands against her chest like a starving person grasping an empty bowl, knowing it would never be filled again. His body lay lifeless on the mound. She remembered screaming so loud the entire tribe drew silent. "I love you."

Her mind jerked out of the memory. Now in the present, she quivered, gasping, face wet with tears. "No." Briskly wiping tears from her eyes with her fisted hands, she drew in a deep breath. "Long ago, in a young, rough world, you had to live as a tribe to survive." Lifting her head high, she vowed, "But now, Tuathal Tachtmhar, king of a thousand heroes, your champions and war band are no match for me, Anwen of Ynys Mon, Captain of the Erinn Pirates." Spurting into a hard run, her foot prints covered those of the war band's ponies as she headed for the rath. Huffing, as she ran across the sand, she swore, "Never again."

She stopped at the *rath*. Running inside the round house, she called out to Riona. "I have no time to explain, but I need a basket full of golden wheat."

Riona grabbed the huge clay jar where she kept the ground wheat for making bread, poured it in a wicker basket, and handed it to Anwen. "Where are you going?"

"To the gods."

Riona's brows arched. "We are all going to the gods. I mean where are you going now?"

"To the copse of trees on the hill, to pray to goddess

Arianrhod. She likes wheat." Anwen shook the wicker basket.

Riona's eyes widen in a baffled expression, but instead of asking more questions, she said, "I'm coming with you."

"My thanks, I may need your wisdom, but hasten."

Anwen ran out of the rath, sprinting toward the hill and up the dirt path that led to the sacred copse. Her steps slowed as her breathing became harder and her legs tired of running up the steep hill. Drawing in deep breaths, she slowed the erratic hammering of her heart as she and Riona entered the copse of ancient oaks.

Clutching the wicker basket of wheat, she faced the oldest gnarled oak. She was glad Riona came with her. The druidess could help. Anwen didn't know if Goddess Arianrhod would listen to her or not. Kaeso was a Roman after all. Riona might know how to persuade the goddess. If Arianrhod wouldn't help her she didn't know what else she could do to save her man.

The ancient wisdom vibrating from the tree renewed her energy. She took a deep breath and flashed a quick smile at Riona, who stood at her side. "Should I begin?"

Riona nodded as she stepped closer to her so that their shoulders brushed against each other.

With both hands on the basket, Anwen lifted her arms high and chanted, "Arianrhod, goddess of the gleaming moon, keeper of the silver wheel of life and death, accept this grain as my bequest."

The moon shone brighter and moved lower, closer to the earth. She glanced at Riona, who had lifted her arms to the goddess as well. Anwen knew her friend used her druidess knowledge to concentrate on the visage of Arianrhod. Anwen gasped as Riona's body began to spasm. Suddenly it stopped.

Anwen looked at Riona's eyes, now fathomless and a paler shade than usual, and realized her friend had fallen into a trance. The goddess had entered Riona's body.

"Arianrhod, I give to you, as you give to me." Anwen placed the basket of wheat down at Riona's feet.

Arianrhod animated Riona's body and spoke through her. "Maiden of the Celt, by what dire need do you summon me forth from Caer Sidi?"

"For a Roman I love." She laced her fingers together and pressed her hands against her chest. "He is to be sacrificed."

With the spirit of Arianrhod controlling her, Riona flipped her long hair against her back with a toss of her head. "They have their own gods. I cannot help you."

Anwen swallowed hard. "His soul came to and from Caer Sidi. Chosen as a god king and sacrificed centuries ago, he returned as a Roman in this life to be with me. She peered deep into the eyes of her friend, still possessed by Arianrhod. "Now the Arch Druid of Tara will give him to the gods because he is Roman."

"I have seen such before. Listen, daughter of the Celt, neither you nor your lover will recall your stay in the Otherworld between rebirths. But while you were both there, you must have been chosen for a second life before him. He wanted to come back with you, but it was not his time. Insisting on rebirth, to be with you again, he chose to come back then, the only way he could, which must have been as a Roman." As she spoke for the goddess, Riona folded her arms across her chest. "Was he captured in battle?"

"No, I brought him ashore." Anwen fought her swirling emotions to try to understand what the goddess revealed. "I captured a ship he was on."

"You pirate Roman ships?"

"Yes. I meant to kill him, but once I gazed at him, I

couldn't." Remembering her attempt to slay him when they first met, brought a tear to Anwen's eyes and she choked back the sob.

"No one can kill the lover they are destined for." Arianrhod fluttered Riona's hand in the air. "It is not possible. We, the gods, have made it so. But god kings are no longer chosen and he was not captured in battle, the Romans are not invading Erinn, so why has the Druid called for your lover to be sacrificed?"

"Because he is Roman." Anwen shrugged. "Kaeso risked all to be reborn, even went so far as becoming a Roman, just to find me again. He loves me."

The goddess shook Riona's head. "This druid reminds me of God Math. I do not like these men who deem they have the right to make decisions about how others live their lives."

Anwen rubbed her forehead as she recalled the tales of Arianrhod the druids had taught her as a child. When the high druid, God Math, tested the goddess' virtue, to see if she was chaste, he touched her belly with his finger and she birthed two sons. "Goddess, do you speak of the birth of your children, the gods Lugh and Dylan?"

"I do. God Math had no right to test my virginity and cause me to birth unwanted children. Neither should this druid sacrifice your man, even if he is a Roman."

Joy bubbled in Anwen, knowing the goddess would not let the druid slay Kaeso. "My thanks, Arianrhod, Keeper of the Silver Wheel, I knew you would save him."

"I cannot do it." Possessed by the goddess, Riona crossed her arms over her chest.

"You will not help me?" She felt screams of frustration and bewilderment at the back of her throat. "Goddess, you must. We don't sacrifice god kings anymore. I think Cairbre gazed into his scrying bowl and saw Kaeso's past sacrifice and mistook it for a vision of the future. Mayhap, he reasons the gods called for Kaeso's sacrifice. You and the other gods took him from me the first time, so you all better save him now."

Riona inclined her head as the goddess spoke through her. "You must do it yourself."

"How?" Anwen leaned her neck back and tried to pull her spinning thoughts and emotions together.

"Shut your eyes."

Anwen squeezed her eyes tight.

"You will see images as in a dream. When they stop, go to Cairbre and have him interpret this dream. This will save your lover." Arianrhod's voice was a calm yet steadfast tone.

With her eyes shut, Anwen let the raging emotions roll off her. Her mind stilled and a mellow warmth engulfed her. Images appeared just as Arianrhod had said. When the vision ended, her eyes fluttered open.

Riona pressed one hand against each side of her face, breathing heavily. Her eyes were no longer the pale ice-blue of a trance. "I feel so tired. I do not remember anything."

"The goddess spoke through you and told me what to do." Anwen smiled, more grateful than she'd ever been for her friend's druid talents. "Come, we must ride to Tara."

She wrapped her arm around Riona to help her walk in her state of exhaustion. Anwen wanted to speed down the hill to the stables, but she kept her pace slow until Riona's strength returned. Once they reached the stable, she saddled and mounted a shaggy white horse. Riona swung onto her steed and followed Anwen in a hard gallop over the green ridge of Tara to the hill fort.

Reining in her mount, Anwen jumped down from the saddle and rushed into the grand hall. She heard Riona's heavy footsteps at her heels. A guard halted Anwen with his long spear. Holding the deadly point no more than a hand's length from her heart.

THE KING'S spear men had dragged Kaeso down the steps under the grand hall into a dark hallway and into a pen in the corner. His cell was fashioned of tall in-ground poles, one next to the other, forming a square with a wood gate in front. They threw him there and stabbed a lit fire brand into the dirt for light and warmth, his only luxury. A pelt or wool cloak to lie on wasn't offered. The King's men shut the gate and wrapped an iron chain around it, caging him in. He dropped to the bare dirt floor and crossed his legs in a seated position. He flung his head back and shut his eyes. He tried to ignore the musky stench so much stronger than the odor in Anwen's *southerrain*.

With nothing to do but wait for death, his thoughts overcame him. He recalled the last basement chamber he'd been held in. Something about the particular memory of Anwen slipping on the ladder, nagged at him. Anwen always stood tall and moved with such grace. Confidence shone from her but that day she was not herself. Why was she so shaky, so awkward at that moment?

He'd asked her what she meant when she'd said, "no matter how much I think I know you or knew you?" He rubbed his chin. She hadn't answered him. Instead she queried him on why he'd asked her about God Kings.

His muscles clinched and his heart raced. She'd known, even then...when she brought him food in the *southerrain*. Even knowing how deeply they loved each other in a previous life, she'd wanted to send him away. Anwen would have sent him off in a tiny ox-hide boat to Londinium if the King's men hadn't overtaken them and captured him. He took a deep breath and scrubbed his forehead. How could she. Even if the war band hadn't taken him to be sacrificed by the druid, there was no hope for them. This great love that span time was one sided.

Why? What had happened to her in this life that had made her so hard, so cold to love. His life would end with him knowing he meant so little to her that even with the intense memories of their previous life together...she could send him away.

SIX

Anwen stared at the black, iron spear point trying to catch her breath as she heard the King call out, "Let her enter."

Afraid the king might change his mind, she swung her arms in a brisk walk toward the head of the hall. She came to an abrupt halt before Tuathal Tachtmhar. His broad, muscular body filled out the oaken throne and his piercing eyes peered back at her.

She bowed to him. "King of Tara, I come to ask for the Roman, but first I need to speak to Cairbre about a troubling dream that came to me."

As Tuathal Tachtmhar leaned forward, he adjusted the crimson cloak draped over his long tunic adorned with embroidered bands of purple, red, and blue. "You say you have come for the Roman." His thick, red brows arched. "You kill Romans, do you not?"

With a tilt of her chin she looked at the King, eye to eye. "He is my slave." *He is my destiny.* "Mine."

"I am your King, not one of your crew. I have a say in deeming what is yours." Tuathal Tachtmhar rubbed his firm chin. "One of your men told me of this Roman slave."

She placed her hands on her hips. "Starn betrayed me."

"It is so." The King nodded toward a circle of men near the throne. Druid Cairbre stood among them, as did Starn, who bowed his head in shame.

She glared at the man who had pirated with her for so long. "Why did you not come to me so I could explain?"

Starn turned his head away, ignoring her.

Her gaze was drawn back to Tuathal Tachtmhar as he peered at her.

With a dignified air of calm and self-confidence, the King added, "Arch Druid Cairbre drew on the power of Lia Fail, the stone of destiny, and scried the will of the gods. They commanded him to sacrifice the Roman at the Lughnasa festival two moon rises hence."

Turning to the circle of men, she pierced the druid with a hard gaze. Knowing exactly what to say, she stretched out her arms to Cairbre. "Master Druid, great seer of dreams, I entreat you to use your gifts to interpret a vision, which has plagued me for three moons."

Caribe stepped toward her. "Tell me your dream." He bore his gaze into her as if he could peer into her soul.

"A hare jumps into a grapevine and eats its fill. A Roman hound pounces on the hare and devours it. The hound gets tangled in the grape vine. A grape drops to the ground, then sprouts into another vine." Anwen paused to catch her breath. "It blooms a flower that is shaped like the hare's face. It wilts, and falls to the ground. The Roman hound frees himself from the first vine and carries away the wilted hare-flower in his teeth. Druid, you, King Tuathal Tachtmhar, and Riona are in my dream as well, dressed in the finest gold brocade, all gathered around a cauldron of black pudding at a wedding feast." Anwen shrugged. "That is all I see, then I wake up."

Cairbre held her in his gaze as he fondled his silver mustache. "The hare is the token of Andraste, Boudica's patron goddess, who watches over the survivors of Ynys Mon. The grape vine symbolizes the Roman Kaeso. The hound is danger. Andraste warns us from the Otherworld." Cairbre reached his arms to the wooden rafters and in a vibrating tone declared, "It is not a human sacrifice we shall have this Lughnasa but a wedding feast." He turned to Anwen. "You must marry the Roman Kaeso. The gods have spoken."

A cry of relief broke from her lips. A warm, bubbling sensation of joy flowed through her. It had worked. The images Arianrhod placed in her mind served her well, as the goddess planned. Kaeso would live.

"So be it." Tuathal Tachtmhar raised his hand to seal the proclamation. "Anwen, accompany Druid Cairbre to the Roman's pen."

Steeling her composure, she held in the joy that threatened to overflow and reveal her farce to the druid. She followed him through a large oaken door at the end of the hall. From there he led her down the wooden steps and to the pen. Cairbre pulled off the iron chains and threw the bolt.

Anwen flew into Kaeso's waiting arms.

"Sweet Venus, you have come to bid me farewell afore my death. Happens you love me after all."

"I have loved you for all time, but I have not come to say goodbye." Tears of joy welled in her eyes and bright laughter burst from her. "You are set free."

She glanced at Cairbre. Getting the silent message, the druid turned and walked away, giving them privacy.

"Cairbre interpreted my dream to mean the gods want you free."

"You saved my life," Kaeso began. "The druid meant to choke my breath from me as a sacrifice to the gods. I kept dreaming it had already happened."

"So it had, once, but never again." Anwen gazed into the depths of his eyes. "The druid also deciphered my dream to mean we must wed." Her pulse raced with joy and excitement "It is the will of the gods."

Kaeso rubbed his chin as his brow crinkled, as if trying to grasp it all. He drew in a deep breath. Suddenly, his eyes gleamed with an inner light of understanding. "Not only has my life been spared, I also have you. By Jupiter, we shall wed!" His whole face spread into a smile.

"Yes." She leaned against his shoulder as he lowered his head.

His warm mouth covered hers and a jolt as strong as a bolt of lightning surged through her. He thrust his velvet tongue between her parted lips and swept it inside her mouth, stroking her to ecstasy. Every pore of her body burned as the kiss deepened.

TWO DAYS LATER, Anwen stood before Tuathal Tachtmhar, King of a thousand heroes, with her head crowned by a garland of white harebells, tiny pink rosemary blossoms, sprigs of lavender and shamrocks. Their sweet scents danced in the air through the halls of Tara. Inside the grand hall, Anwen spun around in glee. The long tunic of green was soft against her skin and the border of gold streamed across it as she turned this way and that, scanning the faces of the massive crowd gathered for the wedding feast.

The chaplet of flowers on her head nearly fell off as

Kaeso pulled her into his muscular arms and gazed into her eyes. "When we first began our voyage of love, I was alone with you, now look at the crew which gathers around."

"An army of well-wishers." Anwen found herself distracted by the way Kaeso's broad shoulders filled out the crimson tunic. As she thought of the muscles rippling beneath his wedding attire, her pulse quickened. "But all I need is you."

"We may need a few more for our crew."

"Are you speaking of children?" She had given up the thought of having babies of her own after the Romans attacked her. Now, she realized she could be a mother. Even now she might carry Kaeso's child within her. A warm tingle ran down her spine.

"Something more immediate." The corners of his lips lifted into a mischievous grin. "I've been thinking, we should take the Roman ships you captured and trade fine Erinn long swords along the coast of Gallia, Germainia, Iberia, even to the Picts of Caledonia."

"Husband, that is a perfect plan." Adrenaline pumped through her at the thought of adventure and love, blended into voyage across the wild sea. "When do we sail?"

"After our wedding night. I'm not going anywhere until then." His eyes burned with a sensuous light.

Her body shivered from the heat of his sexual magnetism. Grabbing his shoulders and rising on her ringbedecked toes, she brushed her lips against his. He ran his fingers down her hair as the rush of his breath blew hot against her ear. In one fluid motion, his warm, wet lips covered hers. His clinging lips tugged and pressed against hers. The drawn out kiss sent the pit of her stomach into a wild swirl.

She heard Cairbre calling out to them. "It's time for the

ceremony. Halt the kiss long enough for me to wed the two of you."

Anwen thought, *Is he addled? I cannot stop.*

Kaeso dragged his lips back and forth against hers in a fervid caress. She burned with need as he wrapped his arms around her and crushed her tighter to him. Basking in the invigorating warmth of his skin, she inhaled his alluring scent. The long, hard kiss sent a path of fire straight to her core. Gently, their lips parted.

The druid seized the moment to swiftly wrap a strip of muslin around Anwen and Kaeso's wrists, fastening their hands together. "Anwen, do you bind your life path to Kaeso's?"

Her throat tightened as she excitedly replied, "Yes."

The druid shifted his gaze to the groom. "Kaeso, do you bind your life path to Anwen?"

"I do."

In a melodic tone, Cairbre commanded, "Both of you say after me, you and no other."

After they repeated the words, the druid turned to the gathered crowd and announced, "This man and woman are bound as one, now and evermore."

SEVEN

The moment the druid pulled the muslin cloth off their writs, Kaeso wrapped his arms around Anwen. Her soft, hot body melded into his. He hungrily covered her mouth with his. The subtle, slightly salty taste of her lips was intoxicating. As he lifted her into his arms, his heart pounded. Holding her snugly, he carried Anwen to the round house, which was empty of Riona and the others. He pushed the door flap aside and carried her to the pallet draped with a bull hide. He lay her down and joined her there, covering her warm, shapely body with his.

She quivered beneath him as her generous curves molded to the contours of his lean, hard body. Reclaiming her lips, he crushed her to him as his tongue explored the recesses of her mouth. Anwen let out a soft gasp of pleasure, giving in to the passion of his kiss. He pulled away for a moment to gaze at her. Anwen's eyes were large and liquid. Her cheeks flushed the color of a wild rose.

Gently, he removed the crown of flowers from her hair, setting it on the chest beside the pallet. He grabbed the belt tied around her waist, unraveled the knot, and dropped it.

He clutched the cloth at the neckline of her green tunic, slipping it off over her head, then tossed it to the floor. After admiring her slender neck and ivory shoulders, her creamy, pink-tipped breasts captured Kaeso's gaze. As he cupped the lush mounds, his hands tingled with heat. He pressed his fingers into her soft flesh, squeezing each mound. Responding to his touch, she thrust her chest forward. Anwen's tight buds hardened beneath his fingertips as he gently rolled the erect nipples. Leaning his head down, he whisked one with his tongue. She moaned.

Kaeso rose from the bed, slipped his tunic off, and threw it down. Moving to the end of the pallet, he leaned down, grasped her shapely thighs and spread them apart, focusing his eyes on the nest of tiny red whorls and the pink nether lips of her pussy. He climbed onto the pallet and reached out, touching the wet folds. The tiny muscles of her sex pulsated with need, dancing for him. Kaeso brushed his thumb over her clit. Anwen whimpered as he stroked her. As she arched her hips, he slid a finger into the hot, wet slit. He pushed his finger in and out as he watched her squeeze it and draw it deeper. She gasped as he pulled out his finger and then slipped two into her tight passage, again thrusting them in and out. She began to pant. His fingers were drenched with her juices. Withdrawing his fingers, he buried his face in her pussy. He licked the pink folds, lapping at her sex as she writhed and mewed.

Lifting his head, he wrapped his fingers around his hard arousal and rubbed the point against the creases of pink flesh. Anwen arched for him. What torture. After waiting a thousand years to marry her so he could take her like this every day, an explosive need over took him.

Grasping her hips tightly, Kaeso drove into her with one

fierce thrust. "You are my captive, at my mercy now, Captain."

Anwen replied with a moan of ecstasy.

As her slick, hot pussy contracted around his cock, he felt it swell even larger inside her. Wracked with fervid need for release, he ground into her. Kaeso drew out all but the head of his erection, and as she gasped, he sunk deep into her. With his breath rushing in hard pants, he slid in and out in the same rhythm.

Her round, jiggling breasts caught his gaze. Capturing a hardened nipple between his fingers, he pinched it hard. She gasped. She raised her legs, resting the heels of her feet on his shoulders.

Faster and faster he pumped her mercilessly. Sweat broke out on his body. In a strained voice, he rasped between pants, "I can't get enough of you. You're going to kill me." Bright lights danced in his head as he pounded into her.

"Maybe that's the plan, but it will be a slow death." Anwen bucked against him.

Her pussy grabbed his cock even tighter, clenching with all her might. As much as the tight walls clamped down on him, he managed to slip out, just to ram her higher and faster each time.

Kaeso's pleasure crested. He groaned long and low in breathless ecstasy. He burst inside her as his whole body quaked. For a few moments, he didn't know where he was or who he was. Surge after surge of intense pleasure over took him.

Anwen's body trembled beneath him as she whimpered in climax.

He pulled out of her snug warm pussy. It was drenched with their mingled juices. He pushed to a standing position and moved to the end of the pallet. He rasped, "Remember, just as I was your slave, you are mine now. What position do captives take before their masters?"

"They kneel," she answered, still panting for breath. Her legs shook as she rose to her knees in front of him.

He gasped at the touch of her wet tongue as she swirled it over his cock. He pushed deep into her mouth. He tangled his fingers in her silky red hair as she rocked her mouth up and down his erection, which swelled and hardened once more.

He loved the wet heat of her mouth wrapped around his flesh. Sucking hungrily, she milked his cock until he moaned in agony. "I have to have you now." Kaeso drew out of her mouth.

"I love the captive play." Anwen rose to her feet and impaled him with her smoldering gaze. "But it's time for that boat to dock. I'm taking over this ship now."

THE DESIRE GLEAMING in Kaeso's clear blue eyes heightened her need. "Now it's my turn to be master and you are the slave. Lay on your back."

"Yes, my captain." In a graceful, fluid motion, he dropped onto the pallet.

Anwen peered at his long body rippling with muscles and glistening with sweat. She dragged her gaze across his broad shoulders, his bulging biceps and his sharply defined chest. The musky, tantalizing scent of his arousal billowed around her.

She fixed her gaze on his long, thick cock, so straight and hard. Her breath grew shallow and she swayed on her feet for a moment, woozy with need. She longed to wrap her pussy around his cock and swallow it whole.

Anwen lowered her body over Kaeso's. She spread her thighs, straddling him. Her pussy hovered over his luscious erection. A sultry heat coursed through her and she licked her lips. She met his gaze. Time stood still as they peered deeply into each other's eyes.

"In truth, in this lifetime, I think I'll keep you alive." She slid her fingers around the girth of his hot, smooth flesh. She rubbed the head of his cock against her slit. "Keep you around, to couple with." She grinned. She positioned the tip of his erection insider her.

His eyes were hooded with desire as he drew in quick, sharp breaths.

She gasped as she pushed down, taking him fully into her.

"Lady, you are in for a long, hard ride." He grasped her hips, digging his fingertips into her flesh.

"I am looking forward to it." She threw her head back as she slid up and down his hard flesh in a slow, sensual rhythm. "The ride of a lifetime...with you."

Kaeso groaned with pleasure.

AFTERWORD

Thank you so much for reading Timeless Voyage. My main reason in writing this novella was to sweep you away to first century AD Ireland and introduce you to the ancient Celts as well as the characters from my mind – Anwen and Kaeso – to include you in their adventures and most importantly... their love.

I hope you enjoyed the magic,

Cornelia Amiri

DEAR READER

Dear Reader,

Thank you so much for reading Timeless Voyage. I hope you had as much fun reading my historical, fantasy, Irish, pirate romance, as I had writing it.

I love pirates. So, inspired by the Irish female pirate captain, Grace O'Malley, I wrote Timeless Voyage about a female pirate, and set it in the Irish Iron Age.

I hope you enjoyed the romance, adventure, and magic of this timeless love story. And that it swept you away to ancient Ireland with Anwen and Kaeso. Because it's readers like you that make writing worthwhile.

Thank you,
Cornelia Amiri

ABOUT THE AUTHOR

The Celtic Warrior Queen made me start writing professionally. I love history and in reading a book about the dark ages, I came across the rebel queen. She inspired me so much. I started jotting down notes, but they were fiction, visions of me involved in the Boudica revolt. Before I knew it, I had accidentally written a rough draft for a novel. And I've been writing books on purpose ever since. Drawing on my love of a happy ending, I have currently penned 35 published romance books.

I live amid the hustle and bustle of humid Houston, Texas with my muse, Severus the Cat. When not writing, I love to read, watch movies, and attend comic cons. I am working on a sequel to Rare Finds, and a sequel to The Brass Octopus, which I am also renaming and republishing as The Librarian and the Rake.

The Lynx and the Druidess

To Love A London Ghost

The Ghost Lights of Marfa

Starry Conquest

As Timeless As Magic

As Timeless As Stone

The Brass Octopus

I Love You More

Forged of Irish Bronze and Iron

Reach

A Boomer Chick's Bingo Card

Love AI Style - Bundle

Swords and Roses - Bundle

Warrior Hearts – Bundle

Need Fire - box set

Dancing Vampires - Box Set

Druidry and the Beast – full series

A Fine Cauldron Of Fish

ACKNOWLEDGMENTS

Acknowledgments

I want to acknowledge my wonderful editor, Michelle Levigne. I appreciate her hard work and talent so much. I also want to thank Julie Darcy for the gorgeous cover art. This book wouldn't be the same without Michelle and Julie.

www.ingramcontent.com/pod-product-compliance
Lightning Source LLC
Chambersburg PA
CBHW051304160726
47994CB00003B/1307